DISC...

DICK WHITTINGTON

DICK
WHITTINGTON

Retold by Kathleen Lines

Illustrated by

Edward Ardizzone

HENRY Z. WALCK, INC.
NEW YORK

```
398.2    Lines, Kathleen
  L          Dick Whittington; retold by Kathleen
         Lines; illus. by Edward Ardizzone.
         Walck, 1970
            48p.  illus.

            Background notes: p.46-48
            The well-loved story has been
         delightfully illustrated in this
         historically accurate text.


         1. Whittington, Richard  2. Great
         Britain -        ◯    Folklore  I. Illus.
         II. Title
```

This Main Entry catalog card may be reproduced without permission.

Text © Kathleen Lines 1970
Illustrations © Edward Ardizzone 1970
All rights reserved
ISBN: 0-8098-1172-3
Library of Congress Catalog Card Number: 75-126975
Printed in the United States of America

Long ago, when Edward III was King of England, there
lived in the West Country a little boy whose name was
Dick Whittington. Dick was poor and quite alone in
the world, for his parents died when he was very young
and he had been left to run about the countryside as free
and wild as a colt. He found shelter from the weather
and a place to sleep where he could; his clothes were
rags and he was often hungry, because, although the
village folk were good to him, they were poor themselves and at times could give him only scraps or a hard

5

crust of bread. There were days when he had no dinner
—and no supper either.

But for all this Dick was a bright lad. He was always
ready to learn more about the world which lay beyond
the country fields and lanes. Wherever people gathered
together to talk Dick would be there listening. On a
Sunday he would get as close as he could to the farmers
where they sat on the tombstones in the churchyard,

waiting for the parson to come. While the barber worked, Dick listened to the news his customers told each other and, once a week for sure, Dick could be found leaning against the sign-post of the Inn where travellers stopped on their way home from the market town. And so, keeping his ears open, he heard a great deal about the far-away city of London. How he wished he could go there!

In those days, to the country people, London was a very gay place, with music and singing and dancing all day long, a place where everyone was splendidly rich and prosperous. It was even thought the very streets were paved with gold. Dick had once seen a golden coin and knew what a deal it would buy, so he

longed to get to London. He thought if he could just pick up a bushel of gold from the streets he would have enough for the rest of his life. And as time went by he became more and more determined somehow to get to London to seek his fortune.

At last his chance came. One day in early summer, when Dick was by the sign-post at the cross-roads, a waggon came through the village, carrying a great load of bales and bundles and packets. It was drawn by eight

fine horses, all with bells at their heads, and the waggoner walked alongside. Dick plucked up courage to
ask if the waggon was on its way to London, and if he
could go too. When the man heard that Dick had no
parents, and saw by his ragged clothes that he could
be no worse off than he now was, he said Dick might
walk with him if he had a mind to. So on they went
together.

The way was long, up hill and down, through

villages and woodlands, and miles of open country, but
at last they reached the gates of the great city. Dick,
with a wave to the waggoner, ran off as fast as his legs
would carry him, in search of the streets paved with
gold. He ran and he ran. Poor Dick, he was soon quite
lost. He ran up one twisting alley-way and down another, and although there was mud and muck aplenty,
there was never a sign of gold. When he came out to
broader streets, dodging this way and that through the
crowds of people, he found the roadway paved indeed
but with rough uneven stones. Look as he would he

could find no sight of gold. Miserable and tired, he ran about till night came, then he curled up in a corner and cried himself to sleep.

Early next morning Dick was wakened by the clatter and bustle of the city at the beginning of another day. Doors and shutters banged, and there was much calling and shouting. People hurried by, riding and on foot; a rowdy band of young lads fought each other with sticks and staves, carts creaked and rattled as their wheels turned noisily over the rough stones. Dick had never heard such a din in his life. For a moment he wondered

where he was. Then he remembered. He remembered
too that there was no gold lying in the streets, that he
was all alone, that he had no money and that he was
very, very hungry. Timidly he began to beg for a half-
penny to buy something to eat, but everyone was in a
hurry and no one would listen to him.

At last a good-natured gentleman stopped and spoke
to him. "You look hungry," he said. "Why don't you
go to work?" Dick explained he did not know how to
set about finding anything to do. "Well, come along

with me then," said the man, and he took Dick off to nearby fields where they were making hay. Here the lad worked briskly and lived merrily, till all the hay was turned and stacked. But after that Dick was just as badly off as before. He wandered miserable and alone, hardly knowing or caring what he did, and too frightened and hungry to take an interest in all the strange, new sights around him. Then one day, being quite faint from lack of food, he turned off busy Cheapside and crept into the doorway of a nearby house.

Now, for good luck or ill, Dick was at the entrance to the house of a wealthy merchant, Mr Hugh Fitz-Warren. The cook, who was preparing dinner, saw him from the window, and called out roughly, "What are you doing there, you lazy rogue? Take yourself off, or I'll give you a sousing with scalding dish-water." But, just at that moment Mr FitzWarren came home, and when he saw a dirty ragged boy lying at his door, he said, "Why do you lie there, my lad? You seem old enough to work, so I fear you must be an idle fellow."

"No, indeed, sir," said Dick, and he tried to get up, but from weakness fell back again. "I would work had I known who to apply to, but now I believe I am very ill for want of food."

Then the kind merchant, seeing his real distress, called his servants to take the boy into the house and give him a good dinner. After he had consulted with his wife, Dame Matilda, Mr FitzWarren said Dick was to be kept on as scullery boy, and to do what he could to help the cook, in return for his board and keep.

So Dick turned the spit, scrubbed the pots and pans, fetched the water and ran errands for the cook. He would have been happy enough in this good household if it had not been for the cook. She was an ill-tempered

creature, and she nagged at him and scolded him from morning till night, and often beat him about the head with a broom, or with anything else that came to hand. However, when Miss Alice, Mr FitzWarren's daughter, discovered the cook was being cruel, she spoke sharply to her and told her she must use the boy more kindly. Miss Alice found some better clothes for Dick, and seeing that he was not a stupid boy, she began to teach him his letters.

With this kindness, and the cook showing less temper, Dick's lot was much improved. But he still had one other misery to endure, for he was plagued every night by rats and mice. These creatures came through the many holes in the floor of his garret room, and ran everywhere, even over his bed. Then one day, a visitor at Mr FitzWarren's gave Dick a penny for cleaning his boots, and Dick went out to see if he could buy a cat. He met a little girl carrying a cat in her arms, and she

agreed to sell it for a penny. "Indeed I am sorry to part with her, for she is an excellent mouser," she added.

Dick ran back with the cat and hid her in his room. He took good care of her and always remembered to carry up tit-bits from his dinner. Puss soon proved her worth; Dick had no more trouble with rats and mice and slept soundly every night.

Now it chanced, soon after this, that Mr FitzWarren's trading ship, *Unicorn*, was ready to sail with a cargo for foreign parts. So, as was his custom, he called all his servants into the parlour to find out what of their own

they would send in the ship for sale or barter, for the kindly merchant thought all his household should have the same chance of good fortune as himself. Everyone had something to send except poor Dick. He had neither money nor goods. Miss Alice would have put down a trifle for him but her father said it must be something of his own.

"But, sir, I have nothing at all of my own, except my cat," said Dick.

"Fetch your cat then, my good boy," said Mr Fitz-Warren, "and send her."

Dick brought down Puss and gave her to the captain, but with tears in his eyes, for he was sad to see her go, and now he would again be kept awake at night by rats and mice.

Everyone laughed at Dick's odd venture in sending out his cat, but Miss Alice, who pitied him, gave him money to buy another.

The attention paid to Dick, and Miss Alice's interest in his affairs, made the cook jealous, and she began to treat him worse than ever before. She beat him whenever she got the chance, scolded him no matter how hard he worked and mocked at him all the time for sending his cat to sea.

At last Dick could bear no more and he decided to run away. So on All Hallows Day, very early in the morning, he bundled up his few clothes and crept out of the house. He walked till he came to Highgate Hill and there he sat down on a stone while he thought which road to take. And while he sat there the six bells

of Bow Church began to chime, and Dick fancied they said:

Turn again Whittington
Lord Mayor of London.

"Lord Mayor of London!" he said to himself. "Why, to be sure, I would put up with almost anything now to be Lord Mayor of London, and ride in a fine coach, when I grow to be a man. I will go back and think nothing of the beatings and the bad temper of the cook, if I am to be Lord Mayor one day." So Dick hurried back, and was lucky enough to reach the house and be about his work before the cook came downstairs.

Meanwhile, the good ship *Unicorn*, with Dick's cat on board, was a long time at sea. She had run into storms and, being blown off course, never reached the port of her destination. Instead, buffeted by contrary winds, she anchored for shelter in a bay on the Barbary coast.

Dark-skinned Moors, the like of whom the English sailors had never seen before, inhabited this country and came to the shore in great numbers to look at the ship. In spite of their surprise to see men so different in colour

from themselves, they treated the strangers with the utmost civility, and showed great interest in the ship's cargo. So the captain sent samples of the best he had on board to their king, who, being much pleased, at once commanded the captain to come to him. Taking the factor who was in charge of the cargo with him, the captain followed the King's servants up to the palace. Here everyone sat on the floor, as was the custom of the country. The rich carpets were covered with designs of gold and silver flowers, and the low tables inlaid with

mother-of-pearl. The King and Queen, who were seated at the upper end of the room, received their visitors most graciously and offered them hospitality.

Vast trays of food were brought in, but scarcely had they been set down, when a crowd of rats rushed in and swarmed over the food helping themselves to almost every dish.

The captain and factor were astonished. "Are not these vermin most objectionable?" asked the captain. "Oh, yes," was the answer, "and very offensive. Not only do the rats eat the King's dinner, as you see, but they come to his bed-chamber and even run all over his bed."

Hearing this the captain remembered Dick's cat. So he told the King that he had a creature on board his ship which would quickly relieve him of the plague of rats. The King's heart heaved so high with joy at this news that his turban fell off. "Run, run," he cried, "and bring this creature to me. If what you say is true I will load your ship with gold and jewels in exchange for it. Such vermin are a dreadful plague at court."

So off went the factor to fetch the cat while another dinner was prepared. He returned just as the dishes were brought in. Once more the rats appeared, and Puss did not wait for bidding but sprang from his arms. In a trice most of the rats were dead at her feet—the

rest in great fright having scuttled away to their holes. The King and Queen were amazed, and delighted too, to be so quickly rid of the vermin, and they asked that the creature which had done them this service should be brought to them. The captain picked up Puss and took her to the Queen. Her Majesty at first started back and was afraid to touch her, having just seen her so savagely at work. But when the captain stroked her, saying, "Pussy, Pussy," the Queen put out her hand and gently touched the cat's soft fur. The captain put Puss down on the Queen's lap, where she played with Her Majesty's hand, purred and then fell asleep.

The King bargained with the captain for the whole of the ship's cargo, at a very good price, and he gave

ten times as much in gold and jewels for the cat as for all the rest put together.

When all business was finished, the captain took his leave, and the weather having improved, he set sail with a fair wind for England.

Mr FitzWarren was early at his desk one morning when, answering a knock at the door, he found the captain and factor come to bring him news of the ship's safe return. After reading the bill of lading, the good merchant raised his eyes to heaven and gave thanks for such a successful voyage. They told him

about Dick's cat, and showed him the great treasure
sent by the King of Barbary in exchange for her.
Mr FitzWarren sent his servants to summon Dick:

"Go fetch him—we will tell him of the same;
Pray call him *Mr* Whittington by name."

When one of the household suggested that such
wealth might be too much for a poor boy like Dick,

the honest merchant replied, "God forbid I should de-
prive him of the value of a single penny. It is all his
own, and he shall have it to the last farthing."

Dick, who had been scouring pots for the cook, was
very dirty. When Mr FitzWarren ordered a chair to be
set for him, the poor boy thought all the company were
about to make game of him, and he begged his master

to let him return to his work. But Mr FitzWarren said, "Indeed, Mr Whittington, we are all in earnest. I have sent for you to congratulate you on the success of your venture. Your cat was sold to the King of Barbary for more than I possess in all the world." And he showed Dick the great chest full of gold and jewels that his cat had earned for him.

Poor Dick hardly knew how to contain himself for joy. With tears in his eyes he begged his master to take part of his treasure, saying he owed all his good fortune to him. "No, no," answered Mr FitzWarren, "it is all your own, and I am sure you will make good use of it." Dick then pleaded with his mistress and with Miss Alice, that they would accept a share of his wealth, but they too refused, at the same time telling him how greatly they rejoiced in his good fortune.

But Dick was too generous to keep everything for himself. He gave a present to the captain and to the factor for their work on his behalf, and to the mate and all the ship's crew. He gave presents also to Mr Fitz-Warren's servants, not forgetting even the old cross-grained cook.

Mr FitzWarren then advised Dick to send for a good
tailor, and for a barber and other necessary people, so
that he would be dressed and outfitted as became his
new position. He invited him to stay on and live with
them, until such time as he found himself a better house.

When Dick was washed and well-barbered, with his
hair curled and wearing a fine suit of clothes and with
his hat cocked, he was as handsome as any young man
who visited at Mr FitzWarren's. And, as wealth contri-
butes to a man's confidence in himself, Dick soon

achieved a good deportment and became a gay and
sprightly companion. Miss Alice who had always been
kind to him out of pity now looked on him quite
differently, and she soon fell in love with him. While
Whittington, for his part, did all he could to please her
and needed no persuasion to become her suitor. Mr

FitzWarren, seeing how things were between them, consented to their marriage.

This was a magnificent affair. The Lord Mayor and the court of aldermen, the sheriffs, and most of the richest merchants of London, attended the ceremony and were afterwards entertained at a truly regal feast.

Mr Richard Whittington was now a city merchant. He became a member of the Mercers' Guild which meant that he could deal in silks and velvets and other rich fabrics. He bought a great house near to the river which he furnished in grand style with the finest work of master craftsmen. Here he and his wife Dame Alice lived in happy contentment. And from here Whittington carried on his business and watched the ships set sail for foreign parts laden with cargoes of wool and hides and cheese and beer, saffron, tin and lead.

Being wise and prudent, by this trade he added to the already considerable fortune his cat had brought him, and he became so rich that the nobility, and even the King, borrowed from him when they were in need of gold.

But though he was prosperous, esteemed by his fellow citizens and the friend of princes, he did not forget what it was to have nothing. As he had been

generous to others when his cat brought him wealth,
so he now had thought for those less fortunate than
himself.

The poor and hungry came daily to his door and
were never turned away. He made provision for
abandoned young mothers and their infants, and built

a shelter for the destitute. Even the wretched debtors in prison were objects of his charity. And he gave for the maintenance of hospitals and religious institutions. He was also a patron of art and learning; he built a library, helped to restore famous buildings and had much to do with constructing the great nave of the

Abbey at Westminster. And, being a Master Mercer, he supplied the court with silks and velvet, rich brocade and cloth of gold for state functions, royal weddings and other important occasions.

The bells of Bow Church, which he had heard while still a poor cook's boy, had spoken truly. For Whittington did indeed become Lord Mayor of London. He was Mayor three times and so well did he execute his duties that he has a lasting place in London's history. One

year, during his term of office, plague came to the city and there was great suffering among the poor. Whittington and Dame Alice went abroad visiting the people, taking clothing and food, physic and other comforts to the sick.

He was loved by the poor and held in high regard by the greatest in the land. To three kings he was a loyal servant and trusted friend. When Henry V came

back from the wars with a French princess for his queen, Richard Whittington invited their majesties to a banquet. King Henry, looking at the lavish spectacle arranged in his honour, exclaimed, "Never had King

such a subject!" To which, on this being repeated to
him at table, Whittington made reply, "Never had
subject such a King." And some say, that there and then
he threw upon the fire bonds which recorded the King's

debt to him for many hundreds of pounds, and stead-
fastly refused to accept repayment for this lordly loan.

When the time came that he fell ill and died,
Whittington was mourned as friend and benefactor
by rich and poor alike.

All his wealth he left to the glory of God and for the
benefit of the people of London. He charged the friends
to whom he entrusted his fortune to finish the work
he had begun, and to carry out what he had planned:

to rebuild Newgate Prison, to establish a house for clergy, with grants for five poor scholars, and to build an almshouse where those who had no home could live for the rest of their lives in security and modest comfort, and to forgive the debts of those who could not easily repay what they owed.

While many marvelled at his generosity, one of his friends, unsurprised, remarked, " While he lived he ever had right liberal and large hands for the needy and the poor."

Richard Whittington's great mansion, and the houses surrounding it, his tomb in the church of St Michael Paternoster Royal, and many of the noble buildings in the city with which he had been connected, were destroyed in the Great Fire of 1666—and so were the bells of Bow Church which had called him back to London. But his provision for the poor remains to this day. His Almshouse, Whittington College, was recently newly erected in the country, not far from London. In the grounds there stands the statue of a ragged boy—a reminder to all of young Dick Whittington, who came alone and penniless to London to seek his fortune more than five hundred years ago.

ABOUT RICHARD WHITTINGTON

Any guide book to the city of London will almost certainly have references to 'Dick Whittington'. It is also almost certain that these references will be a mixture of fact and fiction, for the life-story of a mediaeval merchant has become inextricably entwined with the tale of a poor country boy who was brought great wealth by his cat.

The historical Richard Whittington was three times elected mayor of London (the title Lord Mayor was not then in use), and he died in 1423 bequeathing his fortune to good works and to the poor of London. Plaques in College Hill mark the places where his great house stood and where he was buried. These and a small garden, outside St Michael Paternoster, per-petuate his name and fame, while the legend which has become attached to him assures him a permanent place in folk literature.

Richard Whittington was the third and youngest (and some say illegiti-mate) son of Sir William Whittington of Pauntley in Gloucestershire. The year of his birth is assumed to be 1358 or 1359. Almost nothing is known about his private life and nothing at all about his childhood. Since the family estates were small and impoverished, in all probability Richard Whitting-ton did go to London to 'seek his fortune', and by the time he was twenty-one (in 1379) he was well-enough established to be included in a subscription list of city merchants. It would seem unlikely, accepting these dates, that he served an apprenticeship, as some reference books and some versions of the story suggest, for at that time lads were accepted in their mid-teens and bound for ten years. Whittington did marry 'Miss Alice', but her father, Sir Hugh FitzWaryn, was a wealthy country gentleman, not a London merchant. She had no children and died before 1414.

History records Whittington's advancement in public office, his activities as mercer and merchant-trader and his close association with the crown. In 1396, after the death of the mayor, Adam Bamme, it was Richard II who appointed Whittington, 'in whose fidelity and circumspection we repose full confidence', for the remaining months. He was elected mayor the next year and again in 1406 and 1419. He served the city for the whole of his life, attending a meeting of aldermen only a few weeks before his death.

Other London merchants were wealthy, generous in the endowment of charitable institutions and achieved fame in their own day, and several held the office of mayor more than once. Richard Whittington's success cannot be the reason by itself that a legend grew up about his name. He must have possessed unusual qualities as a man, or there must have been something romantic and spectacular in his career to appeal to the imagination of the common folk amongst whom the germ of the story grew and flourished.

In his specific charitable work Whittington showed considerable imagination. He is credited with giving Londoners a drinking fountain years before any other city had one; the poor of the parish of St Martin Vintry claimed as his gift what may well have been the first public lavatory, the '"Longhouse" . . . beside the Thames and purged by the water at high tide' (mentioned by Miss Imray in a footnote); he built a wing to St

Thomas's Hospital for unmarried mothers; he directed that the inmates of his Almshouse should each have his own place, 'a celle or a litell house with a chymne and a pryvey and other necessaries'; and in his will he expressly cancelled the debts of those who could not easily afford to repay what they owed. He would, one assumes, have been a good master to the apprentices, at one time as many as nine, who not only worked with him but also lived as part of his household.

During his lifetime the poor must surely have looked on Whittington as their friend. Perhaps even then he was 'Dick' to them. After his death it is natural that stories about his generosity should be told and retold, and then added to by conjecture and invention about his youth and origin. And so perhaps the people claimed him as their own, and it was the common folk (disregarding facts as well as probabilities) who changed him into a story-book hero.

The legend of Dick Whittington and his cat is one of Great Britain's most cherished traditional tales. It appeared first in print in 1605 as a ballad: 'The Virtuous Life and Memorable Death of Sir Richard Whittington'; but it must have existed orally much earlier, for this reads not as original invention but the recording of a well-known tale. The story is much as we know it today, with the cat in its vital role ('now this scullion had a cat . . .'), and other apocryphal details; a penurious childhood, the knighthood and the burning of the bonds recording Henry V's debt. Following the ballads the story found a place among the earliest chap-books, and in some form or other has been continuously available for over three hundred years.

It was included by both Andrew Lang and Joseph Jacobs in the first collections of 'fairy tales' each made, and they testify to its anonymous origin. Jacobs wrote: 'I have cobbled this up from three chap-book versions: (1) that contained in Mr Hartland's *English Folk Tales*; (2) that edited by M. H. B. Wheatley for the Villon Society; (3) that appended to Messrs Besant and Rice's monograph.' Lang used 'the chap-book edited by Mr Gomme and Mr Wheatley for the Villon Society.'

F. J. Harvey Darton describes Dick Whittington as 'the strangest of changelings . . . carried from our world into Elfland instead of the other way round.' Even in a field where speculation and argument about origin or derivation is a natural part of investigation, Dick's story has interesting and possibly unique features. It is a universally known nursery tale in which the chief character is a real person, with some incidents true to history, but it is not, and never has been, a 'literary' classic; the ballads had obvious rhymes and lacked imaginative and memorable phrases, while the chap-book versions were roughly written, with picturesque details deriving from the periods in which they were published, considerably later than the story's own date. And, although no one has produced a definitive version or a stylistically polished retelling (de la Mare, for example, used Jacobs' 'cobbled' text), it has happily escaped tedious elaboration. And, lastly, it has no real parallel amongst the folk tales of other countries.

All reputable retellings, by Lang, Jacobs, Ernest Rhys, Mrs Steel, and the version in *The Book of Nursery Tales* (Warne), while differing to a greater or lesser degree, keep to the same basic theme, and they are, with the exception of the last, which is shorter, of almost identical length.

The text of this present edition follows what I believe to be the generally accepted version, with emendations and additions (sometimes only implied) from historical fact. Supported, enriched and reinterpreted by Edward Ardizzone's drawings, the story is set in its correct period, that of the late middle ages, approximately the time of Chaucer.

The last drawing in the book is of the statue in the grounds of Whittington College at Felbridge, from a photograph kindly lent by Miss Jean Imray.

★   ★   ★

The Charity of Richard Whittington by Jean Imray (Athlone Press, 1968)
The Archivist to the Worshipful Company of Mercers gives a detailed, annotated record of the Company's administration of the Trust from 1424 to 1966. Apart from the history itself, there are such fascinating items as :— the Ordinances for the Almshouses; the names of Whittington's apprentices; the rents paid by armiger and tiler, by tawyer, skinner and kerchieflavendre. I owe a great deal to Miss Imray for her patience, kindness and help over many months.
Richard Whittington: The Man behind the Myth by Caroline M. Barron in *Studies in London History* edited by A. J. Kellaway and W. Hollaender (Hodder & Stoughton, 1969)
Original research has revealed much that was not generally known about Richard Whittington, merchant-trader and royal financier. All discoveries are substantiated and the author proposes some interesting theories of her own. Mrs Barron very kindly allowed me to read her essay before publication.
Richard Whittington of Pauntley (published by the City and County of the City of Gloucester: Gloucestershire County Council: The Mercers' Company of the City of London, 1959)
This pamphlet (now out of print) was produced in conjunction with the celebrations in the tiny village of Pauntley of the six hundredth anniversary of Whittington's birth, which was attended by the Lord Mayor of London in full state. It cautiously gives an account of the Whittington family's connections with Gloucestershire. It also describes a sculptured figure holding a cat-like creature, which was uncovered in old cottages in Gloucester city from what was in the fifteenth century called Ratan Row. I am most grateful to the County Librarian and the City Librarian for their kind help.
St Michael Paternoster Royal, Royal College Hill, London, E.C.4
A booklet, obtainable from the church (now the headquarters of the Missions to Seamen), which gives the building's history and Whittington's association with his parish church. The cover is a detail from the Whittington memorial window.   K. L. November 1969